Pure Chance

GILLIAN RUBINSTEIN

WALKER BOOKS
AND SUBSIDIARIES

LONDON · BOSTON · SYDNEY · AUCKLAND

This is a work of fiction. Names, characters, places
and incidents are either the product of the author's
imagination or, if real, are used fictitiously.

First published 1998 by Walker Books Ltd
87 Vauxhall Walk, London SE11 5HJ

This edition published 2004

2 4 6 8 10 9 7 5 3

Text © 1998 Gillian Rubinstein
Cover photograph © Ghislain & Marie David de Lossy/Getty Images

The right of Gillian Rubinstein to be identified as author
of this work has been asserted by her in accordance with
the Copyright, Designs and Patents Act 1988

This book has been typeset in Cochin and Aquinas

Printed in Great Britain by J. H. Haynes & Co. Ltd

British Library Cataloguing in Publication Data:
a catalogue record for this book
is available from the British Library

ISBN 1-84428-941-9

www.walkerbooks.co.uk

*With thanks to Lyn who taught us to ride
and to Helen who lent us Pure Chance*

Chapter one

"You're so lucky," Sarah said. "You've got enough room to keep a pony."

Sarah and Lizzie were exploring Lizzie's new house and garden. The house was in the country, on Piggot Range Road, a few miles from the suburb where Lizzie used to live, and Sarah still lived.

The two girls were best friends, they went to the same school, and they both loved horses.

"And it's just down the road from Jane's," Sarah added, as if that was the reason Lizzie's parents had bought the place.

Neither Sarah nor Lizzie had their own horse but Sarah had riding lessons every Saturday morning with Jane Ramsay, who competed in both dressage and eventing. Sarah had her lessons on an old school horse called Buddy and Lizzie always went to watch. She loved helping Sarah get Buddy ready, and often she was allowed to ride him from the arena back to the yard.

"Dad says I can't have a pony," Lizzie replied. "He says horses are too expensive."

"What a waste, when you've got all this land!" Sarah said, waving an arm towards the paddocks that surrounded the house.

"We've only got five acres," Lizzie said, looking at them in secret delight. The house sat in the middle of the five acres, surrounded by a garden of native Australian shrubs and flowers. There was one flat paddock in front of the house, and two sloping ones behind.

Beyond the back paddocks, the distant sea glinted in the afternoon sun.

"Five acres is enough for a pony!" Sarah called, running ahead to open the gate into the yard.

It did seem a waste, Lizzie thought, to have empty paddocks, full of green grass, and no pony to go in them.

"And you've got two sheds in the yard," Sarah went on. "One could be the feed shed and the other could be the tack room!"

She opened the door to the smaller shed. "Look!" she squealed. "It *was* a tack room, it's got all the hooks and everything."

She lifted the lid of one of the lockers along the wall. "This is where you'd keep your brushes. Oh, Lizzie! Someone's even left a hoof pick behind!"

She held out the little metal hoof pick. "Maybe it's a sign that you're going to get your own pony. This is your first bit of tack."

She stuck her foot out, the sole of her trainer facing upwards. "I'll be the horse. You can practise picking out my feet."

Lizzie picked out Sarah's feet and brushed her with an imaginary brush. Sarah stamped and snorted like Buddy did when he was groomed. Lizzie made a harness out of some old binder twine which was lying on the dusty floor and twisted it round Sarah's shoulders. "Gee up!" she said, and clicked her tongue. Sarah trotted to the front paddock gate, where she stopped and neighed loudly.

Then the neigh turned into a giggle as Sarah glanced towards the house.

"I hope your brothers aren't watching!" she exclaimed.

By the time they were in the paddock, she had given up being a horse. A year ago they might have played horses for the rest of the afternoon, but now it seemed too babyish. So instead of galloping round the paddock they explored it more sedately.

"It's perfect for ponies," Sarah mourned. "It's such a shame you can't have one!"

"I don't really care," Lizzie said. "I love living here even without a pony."

"You should start having lessons with Jane," Sarah said. "Like I do."

"I think even lessons would probably cost too much." There was nothing Lizzie would like more than riding lessons with Jane, but she was sure she wouldn't be allowed to. Sarah didn't have any brothers and sisters, and Lizzie was always having to remind her of how much things cost, and why Lizzie couldn't do everything Sarah did. Her two older brothers both played basketball, and a musical instrument each, and Dad joked that one sport and one instrument was the rule.

The trouble was, Lizzie hadn't found either a sport she really liked, or an instrument that she could play. She'd tried netball and softball and recorder and guitar – but she hadn't been very good at any of them.

Neil was sixteen and wanted to learn to drive, and Scott, who was fourteen, was desperate to go on the school camp. Both boys had enormous appetites and Lizzie's mother was always complaining about how much they cost just to feed.

Moving to a new house was terribly expensive, everyone knew that, but they had to find somewhere bigger; the boys couldn't go on sharing a bedroom, Mum said. And the neighbours kept complaining about Scott's drums and Neil's trumpet, so Dad said, as a joke, that they would find a house in the middle of a paddock.

And they had found the house, in the middle

of three paddocks, on top of the range that divided the suburbs from the real country. But there was no chance that Lizzie was going to get a pony.

Chapter two

"I'm going to cycle over to Jane's and watch Sarah's lesson," Lizzie said to her mother, the following morning. Mum was in the sun-room, which she had turned into a studio. She was working on one of her red-pencil portraits of children.

Lizzie leant over her mother's shoulder and watched. On the table there was a colour photo of a little boy and Mum's eyes darted from the face in the photo to the face that was appearing on her paper.

Lizzie thought her mother was terribly

clever. She wished she could draw, or play a musical instrument, but all these talents seemed to have passed her by. She longed to have something that was all hers, something that she could be really good at.

"Fine," Mum said, adding another couple of strokes to the picture. Then she turned and looked at Lizzie.

"I know you'd love to have lessons too, darling. I'm really sorry we can't afford it. Maybe next year…"

Lizzie's father appeared in the doorway. "Are you ready for coffee? I've just got time for one before I take the boys to basketball."

"Love one!" Mum stretched her arms up over her head and waggled her fingers in the air.

"Do you want to come and watch, Lizzie?" Dad asked.

"I'd rather watch Sarah," Lizzie said.

Dad frowned. "I wish it was basketball you yearned after."

"I'm only going to watch, Dad! I'm not asking you for riding lessons!"

"As long as that's clear," Dad said. "As Mum says, maybe next year."

Next year? It seemed like ages away. Next year lessons wouldn't be any less expensive and Neil and Scott would probably have even huger appetites by then.

Lizzie went outside feeling slightly cross. She opened the door of the larger shed and clicked her tongue.

"Hey, Rainbow," she crooned. "Hey, boy."

Lizzie pretended her bike was a horse. Scott and Neil had rebuilt it over the years, and it was lots of different colours, so she called it Rainbow after Captain Starlight's horse in *Robbery Under Arms*.

She led Rainbow out of the shed, and

checked to see if anyone was watching. She didn't want Scott to see her. He teased her all the time about horses. From the side of the house, next to the carport, came the thud of the basketball. Dad had put up a hoop there and the boys were practising.

Lizzie got on her bicycle, saying nothing, and rode down the driveway. When she got to Piggot Range Road she said, "Gee up, Rainbow!" and began to "trot".

The road had wide sandy verges on either side for horses. Lizzie pedalled as fast as she could. It was downhill all the way to Jane's. Rainbow was as swift as the wind. Lizzie sang loudly, feeling free and happy.

Along the road were several horse properties and livery stables. Since it was Saturday morning they were all humming with activity. Girls were schooling horses in dressage arenas or over jumps. In the yards people were saddling up, grooming, mucking out yards and washing horses.

Lizzie wondered if any of them noticed her. Maybe they thought she was on her way to see her own horse. But not many of them seemed to be wearing jeans and trainers like her. They were all in jodhpurs and black top boots, or brown leather short boots. They all looked quite frighteningly confident as they shouted at each other or at their horses. And the horses obeyed them docilely, as if they were under a spell.

Horses are just magic, Lizzie thought as she got off her bike to cross the road at Jane's place.

Sarah's mother's car was parked outside and Sarah was already in the school arena. Lizzie could hear Jane's voice from the driveway. She was yelling at Sarah. "Legs, Sarah, use your legs on him. No, don't pull on his mouth with your hands. Sit deep and use your legs."

Lizzie grinned. Jane said the same things every week. She undid the gate and went to sit on the side of the arena. Sarah's mother and Jane were standing in the sand in the middle, watching Sarah trot Buddy in a figure of eight.

"Flex his neck!" Jane shouted. "You've got to get him bending before you make the turn. And don't forget your diagonal. Sit two, and then rise."

Sarah sat rather bumpily to the trot.

"Still wrong," Jane said. "Go large and try and get the feel of it."

"Go large," Lizzie mouthed silently. "Wrong diagonal." They were like magic words to her, runes or spells. If only she could have them said over her!

Mrs Chapman gave her a wave and came and sat down next to her. Lizzie was rather scared of Sarah's mother. Mrs Chapman was one of those people who thought there was a right way and a wrong way to do everything, and that she always knew the right way. Everything Sarah did had to be done absolutely properly. She always had to have the right clothes for every occasion. She was beautifully turned out now in black jodhpurs with a red seat, and short brown R. M. Williams boots.

Jane, on the other hand, was wearing very faded old fawn jods, long rubber riding boots and a battered stockman's hat. Her red hair was pulled back in a ponytail. She had pale skin which she tried in vain to keep from freckling, and bright blue eyes.

"Talk to him with your hands," she urged Sarah. "Very gently."

"I'm not sure what you mean," Sarah said.

"Come here. I'll get on him and show you."

Sarah dismounted and Jane got on Buddy.

"Wake up!" she said.

Buddy suddenly looked like a different horse. His back end seemed to come underneath him, he arched his neck and played with the bit. His step became lighter.

"Can you see the difference?" Jane called. She put Buddy into a slow canter and circled round them. "See the bend you can get from him."

"He doesn't do that for me," Sarah complained.

"That's why you have lessons," her mother told her. "So you can learn to do it."

Sarah got back on Buddy again, but she couldn't make him look like Jane did.

"It's hard when you're only riding once a week," Jane said at the end of the lesson. "You're not getting enough practice really."

"Can Lizzie ride Buddy back to the yard?" Sarah said.

"If you give her your helmet," Jane agreed.

Lizzie's eyes went wide with delight. Jane noticed and smiled. She looked at the chestnut, who was sweating a little. "In fact you can walk him round the arena for a few minutes and cool him off."

"Can I?"

Lizzie put Sarah's helmet on with hands that trembled a little. Then she put her foot in the stirrup and swung her leg up. She gathered up the reins. Jane adjusted the stirrups to the right length.

"Squeeze gently with your leg," she said.

Lizzie squeezed. Buddy walked quietly forward. Behind her she heard Jane say to Mrs Chapman, "Are you thinking of getting a pony for Sarah?"

"Oh well, you know, if the right one came along," Mrs Chapman replied. "Of course, we'd have to find somewhere to keep it."

"You could keep it here," Jane suggested. "I've got room for one more horse."

Lucky, lucky Sarah, Lizzie thought. She pretended Buddy was hers. They had just been out for a long ride, and now they were walking home. "Good man," she crooned to him, copying Jane. His ears flicked back at the sound of her voice. He can hear me, she thought. He can feel me! Oh, I do hope he likes me. She tried to make herself look like Jane had looked on the chestnut horse. She tried to make her hands talk to him. His step picked up a little. She could feel his haunches swing.

"That's a nice walk," Jane said as they went past. "You can walk him back to the yard now."

Mrs Chapman had a rather cross look on her face as if she didn't think it was right that Jane should praise Lizzie, who wasn't even paying for lessons.

As Lizzie slid off Buddy's back, Jane said, "You look like a natural. Any chance of you having some lessons?"

Lizzie shook her head. "Dad says they're too expensive."

"What a shame," said Mrs Chapman.

"Funny." Jane grinned at Lizzie. "That's what dads always seem to say. Do you know how to put his rug on?"

"Dad's rug?" Lizzie said. Then she realized Jane was talking about Buddy.

"Come on, I'll show you."

Sarah finished brushing down the chestnut and painted his hooves with grease. Jane picked up the big canvas rug from where it was hanging on the rail, and showed Lizzie how to put it on straight, and do up the leg straps, looping one through the other so they didn't slip. Then she buckled the front strap.

"You can put him in the windmill paddock

now," she said. "Leave his halter on. He's got another lesson this morning."

Buddy followed Lizzie obediently. In the paddock she gave him a carrot. He sniffed at it before taking it delicately with his soft lips, and crunching it up.

"Can I watch the next lesson?" she asked when she returned to the yards.

"Sure," Jane replied.

"Can I stay too?" Sarah pleaded, but her mother said she had to go home as they were going shopping.

"You are lucky living so close," Sarah said. "You'll be able to come here all the time. I have to wait for Mum to drive me."

Lizzie watched Jane give lessons all morning, and helped her with the horses. At lunchtime, she decided she'd better go home.

She cycled back up Piggot Range Road. It was uphill and she was tired, so Rainbow didn't fly like the wind, he just plodded along. Lizzie kept remembering how it had felt to ride Buddy. She looked at all the horses in the paddocks and pretended each one of them was hers.

Chapter three

In the last paddock, just over the road from the driveway to her house, Lizzie noticed a small bay horse standing by the fence. She stopped to talk to him.

She let Rainbow lie down on the ground for a rest. She had one carrot left in her pocket so she offered it to the little horse. He looked at her doubtfully and tossed his head back.

"Come on," she said firmly, in a new Jane-like voice. The horse stepped towards her and took the carrot from her hand. She reached out and patted him on the neck. He angled his head slightly so he could watch her out of his dark brown eyes.

He had a wide white blaze covering most of his face and three white socks. His body was a warm brown colour; his legs were darker, almost black. He was very scruffy. His mane and tail were matted and his coat muddy.

"You need a good brush," Lizzie said aloud. "Doesn't anyone look after you?" What a waste, she thought. Someone owned this horse and didn't look after it, whereas she would love to look after a horse, but didn't own one.

The noise of a car pulling up behind her made her turn round. The car was small and yellow. Out of it clambered a woman who looked about the same age as Jane. She moved a little awkwardly and used a stick.

"Hello," she said. Her face was very thin, and she had dark rings under her eyes, but the eyes themselves, hazel-green, were full of life and warmth. Her voice was warm and friendly too. "You making friends with Spud?"

"Hi," Lizzie said. "Is he yours?"

"I'm afraid so," the woman said. "He doesn't look in very good shape, does he?"

"Is that his name? Spud?"

"His show name is Pure Chance, but I always call him Spud."

"Spud? Why Spud?"

"I don't know. It just seems to suit him." The woman smiled, showing white rather irregular teeth.

Spud put his head forward and nuzzled Lizzie on the arm.

"He likes you," the woman said. "He's very naughty. He's very hard to catch. It's the only thing wrong with him really. I can't ride him any more." She waved her stick in the air to emphasize the point. "I broke my ankle a year ago and it's never healed properly. And no one else can ride Spud because they can't catch him. I don't know what I'm going to do with him."

She was silent for a moment, and then she looked at Spud standing placidly next to Lizzie and allowing the girl to pat him.

"There's a halter on the back seat of the car," she said. "Do you think you could get it and slip it on him?"

"OK," Lizzie said, and went to get the green halter.

"Put the lead rope over his neck," the woman said quietly. "Once you've done that, he'll just stand still. But it's getting close enough to him that's the problem. I can't chase him all over the paddock."

Spud snorted a little when he saw the halter in Lizzie's hand and for a moment she thought he was going to run away. "Stand still," she said in her best Jane-voice, and slipped the lead rope quickly over his neck. He dropped his head towards her and she didn't even have to reach up to put the halter on. She did up the buckle and clipped on the lead rope. Spud didn't budge.

The woman was shaking her head, amazed. "Fancy him letting you do that! Could you lead him over to the gate, and tie him up there? I'll be able to give him a brush now."

"Can I help you?" Lizzie asked eagerly. She had fallen totally in love with Spud, who had let her catch him when no one else could.

"Thank you," said the woman, "I'd love you to. But don't you have to go somewhere. Home? Lunch perhaps?"

"I only live over the road," Lizzie said, pointing to the house, which was just visible through the trees.

"Well, OK then. Thanks! There's a basket of grooming gear on the back seat. Could you carry that over to the gate for me? I'm Moya, by the way."

Lizzie led Spud over to the gate and tied him up. Then she got the grooming things and began to brush him. "Do you live up here?" she asked, wondering if this was Moya's paddock.

"No, I live in the city. I've got a flat near my work. I have to pay to keep Spud here. I try to come every day to check up on him, but since I had the accident it's been difficult."

"Did you fall off Spud?"

Moya laughed. "No, I never fell off Spud all the years I was riding him. I was knocked over by a car. Made a complete mess of my ankle. I've got to go back into hospital soon and have it all reset again."

"How awful," Lizzie said.

"It's made it really hard to look after Spud properly," Moya said, starting to unravel the knots from his mane and tail. Lizzie took her lucky hoof pick out of her pocket and cleaned his feet. His shoes were very worn and one was missing.

"The farrier hasn't been able to shoe him," Moya said. "I must get his feet done. Maybe you could catch him again for me one day?"

"Oh yes," Lizzie said, "if he'll let me."

"I think he will," Moya said. "I can see he really likes you."

Spud leant his head against Lizzie and rubbed her shoulder.

Chapter four

Lizzie couldn't wait to see Sarah at school on Monday to tell her about Spud. But Sarah had even more exciting news.

"Jane's found a pony for me," she burst out as soon as she saw Lizzie. "A friend of hers is selling it, and Jane thinks it would be perfect for me. We're going to look at it after school. Can you come too?"

Somehow Spud didn't seem so important after that.

The pony was a grey mare, called Melody. She was thirteen hands high and twelve years old. Sarah rode her in Jane's friend's field, her eyes glowing.

"She's a good little all-rounder," Jane said. "She's done a lot of Riding Club and a bit of showing. She'd be a perfect first pony for Sarah. But she's not cheap."

Mrs Chapman said, "I don't mind paying the money if it's the right horse."

Lucky Sarah, Lizzie thought. She couldn't believe that Sarah was going to get her own pony, just like that. Sarah didn't even have anywhere for Melody to live. Sarah had a pony and no paddock, while Lizzie had three paddocks and no pony. It didn't seem right.

"Cheer up," Scott told her, when she was complaining about it at home. "Sarah may have Melody, but you've got the famous thoroughbred, Rainbow!"

Lizzie needed all her self-control not to kick her brother on the shin. She wished Sarah could keep Melody at her place, and then they could share her, but Mrs Chapman wanted the new pony to live at Jane's.

After that, Sarah had her weekly lessons on Melody and she rode her after school as well, sometimes in Jane's arena, and sometimes out along the side of the road. Lizzie went with her on Rainbow but, while the bicycle had made a satisfactory horse when she was on her own, alongside a *real* pony it was all too clearly only a bike.

And Sarah seemed to be turning into a different person now she had Melody. She had always been so nice before, but owning a pony had actually made her quite nasty. If Melody shied at a plastic bag in the ditch, or trotted too fast on the way home, somehow it was always Lizzie's fault. It had been fun when both of them were ponyless, and could play horses together. Now that one of them actually owned a pony, things had changed.

There was no question of sharing Melody, either. Once, Sarah let Lizzie ride her in the arena at the end of her lesson. Jane praised Lizzie's riding, and after that Sarah's mother wouldn't let Lizzie ride Melody again.

"Lizzie's not learning to ride properly like you are, Sarah," Mrs Chapman said. "She could spoil Melody. After all, we paid a lot for her, and we don't want her picking up bad habits. And Lizzie might fall off and hurt herself. We don't want that."

"Don't let Sarah's mother upset you," Jane said quietly to Lizzie later. "I've seen it happen heaps of times. Owning a horse is a big responsibility. When people first get their own horse they often get really anxious about everything and it makes them act in a very funny way! Sarah should take Melody to Riding Club. She'll soon get used to her

37

and then she'll settle down."

Riding Club was held on Sunday mornings, on a property a little further along Piggot Range Road.

"You can come too and strap for me," Sarah told Lizzie before her first day there.

Strap. It was another of those magic words. But strapping for Sarah turned out to be not very magic at all.

Sarah rode down from Jane's, and Lizzie had to walk after her, as Sarah said the bike frightened Melody.

There were a lot of horses there, with riders of all ages wearing the blue and yellow T-shirts which were the club uniform. Sarah was put in the junior group. Apart from lunchtime, when Lizzie got to brush Melody and lug a bucket of water from one side of the grounds to the other for her, Sarah rode the whole time, and Lizzie sat and watched.

Not that she minded watching. It was so interesting looking at all the horses and the different riders, spotting who was confident and who was nervous, which were the reliable horses and which ones were likely to spook at everything.

But Sarah ignored her all day and only spoke to her to order her around.

In the morning the juniors practised jumping. Sarah and Melody did not do particularly well. Melody kept running out the side of the jump and once Sarah nearly fell off.

"I can't understand it," Mrs Chapman kept saying to Lizzie. "Melody's meant to be an all-rounder. She doesn't seem to be able to do anything."

Lizzie could have told her that it was not Melody's fault, but Sarah's. She wished Jane was there to give some advice, but Jane was away with her horse, Charlie, at a One Day

Event. And Lizzie couldn't very well tell Mrs Chapman what the problem was. She could see that Sarah was very nervous. She was hanging on tightly to the reins as if she was frightened Melody was going to run away. It was making the little mare uncomfortable and edgy. She kept walking backwards to get away from the heavy hands on the bit. Then Sarah dug her heels in to make Melody go forward.

Finally Lizzie couldn't bear it any longer. She went over and said, "Don't hang on to her mouth so much. Let her go forward." It was exactly what Jane said in every lesson.

Sarah went red. "I suppose you think you know everything," she said angrily. She yanked Melody's head round and rode away.

After lunch they practised novelties. Lizzie knew that Melody was especially good at these, being fast and unflappable. But all the horses got a little overexcited at racing each other, and some of them started to get out of control. Melody came cantering down at the end of the bending race, and Lizzie saw Sarah's face as they shot past. It was tense and pale with fear.

Sarah managed to pull Melody up. She walked her back to where her mother was sitting.

"I think I'll take her home," she said. "She's had enough for one day."

"Lizzie, do you mind walking back with her?" Mrs Chapman said.

So Lizzie walked all the way back to Jane's. Melody was keen to get home and she wanted to trot. Because Sarah wouldn't let the reins out, she began to jog.

"You should make her walk on a long rein," Lizzie said.

"That's what I'm trying to do," Sarah said

with tears in her eyes. "It's because you're walking next to her. You're making her do it."

Lizzie dropped behind and angrily kicked a few stones into the grass. She knew exactly how she would calm dear little Melody down and make her walk back easily and happily. And there was no need for Sarah to be so horrible. After all, she was the one who had the pony now. It was so unfair!

Chapter five

Back at Jane's Lizzie helped Sarah put Melody away. Neither of them spoke.

"Have you two had a fight?" Mrs Chapman said when Sarah was ready to go home. When Sarah didn't answer, Mrs Chapman said, "I expect Lizzie feels a bit jealous."

"I'm not jealous," Lizzie said, but it came out in a very angry way that made her sound as if she was.

"Keeping horses is very expensive," Mrs Chapman said. "And with a big family and both of your parents unemployed it must be out of the question for you."

This made Lizzie even angrier. She got Rainbow from where he was leaning up against the gatepost and cycled off, pedalling as hard as she could to get rid of her rage. Unemployed! Just because both her parents worked at home did not mean they were unemployed! And three children was hardly a big family. I'll go and see darling Spud, she thought as she rounded the last corner, puffing like anything. He'll cheer me up.

The little yellow car was parked on the verge and Moya was standing at the gate. She had a bucket in one hand and Spud was trying to snatch food out of it without coming close enough to be caught.

"Hello!" Lizzie called.

"Oh, Lizzie," Moya said, "look at this rascal." Her voice sounded rather funny and Lizzie suddenly realized she was near tears.

"Have you got to catch him? Is the farrier coming?" Two weeks earlier Lizzie had caught Spud on Saturday morning so the farrier could give him new shoes and worming paste.

"I haven't got to catch him today for any special reason, but I've got to go back into hospital next week for another operation. I don't want to leave him here without anyone to look after him, but whoever looks after him has got to be able to catch him. I hoped if I always brought a bucket of feed with me each time I came to see him, he might get used to being caught. But look at him. He knows I can't run after him!" Moya was silent for a few minutes and then she said, trying to joke, "You'll end up at the knacker's, you silly boy!"

"Oh no!" Lizzie cried.

Spud grabbed another mouthful of food and stood munching. He was so alive and so beautiful. Lizzie couldn't bear the thought of him not being there any more, not chewing the sweet grass, not feeling the warmth of the sun on his bright bay coat.

"I could look after him for you," she said.

"Lizzie!" Moya stared at her. "Your parents wouldn't let you keep him at your place, would they?"

Lizzie was speechless. Moya thought she didn't understand. "I mean, borrow him for a little while. It wouldn't cost you anything. I'd pay for the farrier and his worming paste and all that sort of thing."

"I couldn't ride him too, could I?"

"Yes, of course you could. I've got a saddle and a bridle for him. I'll lend them to you."

Lizzie could feel her heart beating so strongly it felt as if it filled her whole body from her throat to her stomach. Moya was offering to give – well, lend – Spud to her.

Spud, who she adored so much!

"Oh I wish you'd take him," Moya said. "I know he'd be happy with you."

"Let's go and ask my parents," Lizzie said.

Her mother was working in the garden. She looked up in surprise as Lizzie jumped out of the little yellow car.

"Mum, this is Moya," Lizzie said.

Moya struggled out of the car, dropping her stick and picking it up with some difficulty. "I'm a bit of an old crock, I'm afraid," she laughed.

"Come and sit down," Mum said, shooting a questioning look at Lizzie. "I'll make a cup of tea. I'm sure Dad's ready for one too. Lizzie, go and give him a shout."

Lizzie went into the study. "Dad?" she said.

Her father looked up from the monitor. "Hello, chook!"

"Mum's making a cup of tea," Lizzie said, and then she said very quickly, "Dad, there's someone here to see you. She's got something very important to ask you. Dad, I want you to promise not to say no right away."

He looked at her suspiciously. "It wouldn't have anything to do with horses, would it?"

"How did you guess?"

"I've noticed lately it's the only subject that puts that light in your eyes and that grin on your face!"

"Dad, just come and talk to her."

"I'll come for a cup of tea," Dad groaned, "but I can't promise to say yes to anything to do with horses."

The discussion went on all evening, long after Moya had driven off. Mum was rather in favour of the idea of Lizzie borrowing Spud.

"It'll be good for Lizzie, it'll help Moya, and

the horse can keep the grass down in the pad-docks."

"Look," Dad argued, "you start out just borrowing a horse and one thing leads to another. She'll want to ride, won't she? She'll need riding clothes. Then I'll bet you she'll want to start going to this Riding Club Sarah goes to. That'll mean membership fees, uniform, all that stuff. And we don't even know if the horse is safe. After all, no one can catch it."

"I can catch him," Lizzie said. "And Moya said he was a perfect gentleman to ride."

"He's a gift horse," Neil said. "You shouldn't look him in the mouth!" He grinned at them all. "I've been dying to make that joke!"

"Why do you want to look them in the mouth?" Scott said. "I've always wondered."

"It's to find out their age," Lizzie said.

"How old is he?" Dad demanded.

"Moya said he was sixteen."

"Isn't that a bit old?" Dad said. "He'll probably break down on you."

"That's the same age as me!" Neil commented. "Spud's old enough to drive."

"Spud!" Scott repeated. "Catchy sort of name for a horse!"

"His show name is Pure Chance," Lizzie said.

"Show name!" Dad spluttered. "I suppose you'll want to start showing him! You might as well go and stand in the shower and tear up bank notes."

"Calm down," Mum told him. "You're exaggerating everything. Why shouldn't Lizzie take the horse for a little while at least?"

"Mrs Chapman was right," Lizzie said sadly. "She said I'd never get my own horse because you were unemployed."

"Unemployed! What does the woman mean by that? Hasn't she heard of self-employment?" Dad looked outraged.

"And we've got such a large family, there's no extra money," Lizzie went on tragically.

"Three children is hardly a large family," Dad exclaimed. "Far better to have three normal children than one spoilt one. Anyway what business is it of hers?"

"I'm just telling you what she said," Lizzie replied. "And she's right, isn't she?"

"I think Lizzie should have the horse," Neil said. "After all, she doesn't do anything else."

"She's never found her own thing," Mum added. "Maybe her thing is horses."

"It is, it is," Lizzie agreed fervently.

"I think she should have him too," Scott added. "I like the idea of a horse called Spud. Spud is a much cooler name than Rainbow."

This unexpected support was too much for Lizzie. Her eyes filled with tears. "I won't ask you for any money. I'll get a Saturday job. I'll work for you and Mum. I'll look after him all by myself. Please, oh please!"

"Don't start crying!" Dad said. "That's no way to carry on a rational discussion." He looked around the table. "I seem to be outnumbered on this. But what if the horse isn't suitable, or safe? After all, chookie, you don't really even know how to ride."

"None of us knows anything about horses," Mum said. "I think we should get the expert's advice. Maybe Jane could try him out for us."

"You mean you're going to say 'yes'." Lizzie looked from Mum's face to Dad's. "You're really going to say 'yes'?"

"We'll see what Jane says," Dad promised. "But if she doesn't think he's safe, there's no way you're going to keep him, not even as a lawn mower!"

Chapter six

Jane agreed to come over the following day and ride Spud. Lizzie called Moya and told her, and Moya said that was a very good idea, and she would bring his saddle and bridle.

Lizzie was in an agony of impatience all day at school. She didn't want to tell Sarah in case Spud turned out to be unrideable. If Spud turned out to be unrideable she wouldn't be able to have him, and if she didn't have him she was so afraid he might end up at the knacker's. She didn't think Moya would ever do that – she loved Spud too much – but if anything happened to Moya, who would look after Spud?

She didn't want Sarah to know all that. So she said nothing, just listened to Sarah telling their other friends about how brilliant Melody had been at Riding Club, and how she was going to take her to Interclub in the spring.

"And Jane thinks we should enter the Young Rider class in the Dressage Spring Champs as well."

It sounded terribly grand, Lizzie thought. But she didn't care about Interclub or the Spring Champs. She just wanted Spud.

She got off the school bus and saw the little yellow car already outside Spud's paddock. A few moments later Jane's old truck came roaring round the corner.

Lizzie ran to open the gate for her and after Jane had parked and Lizzie had got rid of her school bag, they walked back to the paddock together.

When they got to the gate Jane exclaimed, "Oh, this is the horse!"

"Do you know him?" Lizzie asked.

"No, I've just noticed him when I've driven past. He looked a bit too nice to be standing in a paddock."

"Do you really think so?"

"He looks nice, but it's hard to tell until you actually get on."

Moya got out of the car with even more difficulty than usual.

"Can see why you don't ride any more," Jane said in her direct way.

"I kept hoping I'd get back to it," Moya said. "But I think I've got to accept that I'll probably never ride again. So I've got to find somewhere for Spud."

"He looks rather big for Lizzie. She's got

55

no experience at all."

"He's very easy to ride. He's got no vices. And he's totally safe on the road. The only problem is that he's so hard to catch."

"You're kidding?" Jane watched in surprise as Lizzie walked straight up to Spud and slipped the halter over his head. "That doesn't look like hard to catch to me!"

"Lizzie's the only person who can do that," Moya sighed. "I don't know what it is about her. He just seems to like her."

"Lizzie, lead him over the road and up to the house," Jane said. "We might as well make sure you can handle him on the ground to start with."

"Walk on," Lizzie said to Spud and he followed her out of the gate and over the road. He walked carefully alongside her, not pulling on the rope at all, keeping his head level with her shoulder. He stopped at the gate and waited politely while she opened it. Then he walked on.

He looked at everything, ears pricked forward, his eyes large and alert. He stopped once, when Dad appeared on the ride-on mower, but when Lizzie clicked her tongue at him, he followed her again.

"He seems to have nice manners," Jane said, when they had brushed him and tacked him up. "How long since anyone's ridden him?"

"More than a year," Moya said. "Before that, I didn't do much on him. I work in a bank and my job's been pretty demanding for quite a while now."

Jane walked and trotted Spud slowly to start with, explaining to Lizzie that he would be very stiff.

Then she began to trot him a little faster and turn him in circles and figures of eight.

Spud seemed to float above the ground.

"Wow!" Jane said. "He moves nicely!"

After a few more minutes she rode over to Moya and Lizzie. "This is a very nice horse," she said sounding slightly surprised. "Did you do dressage on him?"

"Not really," Moya said. "I just tried to teach him a few things."

"You did a good job! Lizzie, hop on, and I'll see how you go with him."

Jane adjusted the stirrups and Lizzie, feeling as if she was in a dream, found herself riding Spud.

Jane walked next to her while she got the feel of him. Then she told Lizzie to walk round the paddock and to stop when she said so.

"Sit very deep. You look like a pimple on a pumpkin at the moment, but you'll grow into him. Now, hold the rein, stop your seat moving and just think *Stop*."

And Spud stopped.

"Now a gentle squeeze with the leg and think *Walk*."

Spud walked on.

"She looks awfully small on him," Dad said anxiously when Lizzie had finished riding.

"Yes, he is a bit big for her at the moment," Jane agreed. "But he's a lovely horse. I think she'll be able to handle him. I suspect she'll be a good rider. She'll need some lessons though."

"I knew it," Dad groaned. "The expenses start already. What else?"

"Riding clothes, helmet, boots and so on. She should take him to Riding Club, so uniform, membership, that sort of thing."

Lizzie was watching her father's face. It was getting more and more glum. Spud rubbed his head against her shoulder. She patted him miserably. She knew Dad was going to say she couldn't have him. She couldn't bear it. She loved Spud so desperately. She'd die if she didn't get to keep him.

"On the other hand," Jane went on, "you've got three good paddocks which haven't been overgrazed. It won't cost you much to feed him. And you won't have to buy any tack for him, if Moya lends you this stuff."

"I'll pay for the farrier and any vet bills," Moya put in.

"If you were buying this horse you'd be paying a couple of thousand dollars for him," Jane said.

"That's what Mrs Chapman paid for Melody," Lizzie said, awed.

"Melody's a nice all-rounder," Jane said. "But she hasn't got Spud's movement. Spud is really special!"

Everyone stared at Spud. He stood with his head low, leaning slightly against Lizzie's shoulder. His eyes were half-closed. He didn't look very special at all.

"If Lizzie carries on helping me out on Saturdays and Sundays," Jane said, "I could give her lessons for free."

Dad looked around at the pleading, eager faces. "You'll have to do all the work yourself," he said to Lizzie.

"I will, I will!" she promised, her heart pounding with excitement.

"You won't ask Mum or me to do it for you when it's wet and cold?"

"No! I'll always take care of Spud myself."

"Looks like you've got yourself a horse to look after, then," Dad said. "I must be out of my mind," he added.

"Thank you, thank you!" Lizzie squealed.

Chapter seven

Lizzie's life became extremely busy. Every morning as soon as she woke up she ran outside to say good morning to Spud. She thought about him all day at school and every afternoon she rode him. At first she rode around the paddocks, but as she got more used to him she began taking him out on rides.

Spud was good on the road and never shied at anything, not even noisy motorbikes, or the fodder truck that came rattling up to Jane's once a week with the feed for her horses.

Lizzie phoned Moya almost every day, until

Moya went into hospital for her operation, and they had long conversations about how Lizzie was getting on and what Spud was doing.

Every weekend was taken up with working at Jane's. Spud became quite used to being put in the paddock with Buddy and Melody while Lizzie mucked out the yards, cleaned Jane's tack for her before competitions and events, prepared the feeds for the horses, and groomed them. She never minded how much work there was, even when it was wet and the yards and horses were muddy, for all the time she was learning more and more about how to look after horses. And then she knew how to look after Spud.

Spud and Melody became good friends and were always pleased to see each other. Melody behaved better out on a ride if Spud went too. But Lizzie and Sarah were not quite as close as they had been before either of them had their own pony. A little edge had crept into their friendship.

Jane gave Lizzie a lesson every week and let her practise in the arena. Often she would come out and tell her what she was doing wrong, and it would turn into a lesson without either of them realizing it.

"You and Spud make a great combination," Jane said. "It's fun watching you improve so fast. You'll be able to take him to Riding Club soon. You must start competing him. Then you can enter the Young Rider classes at the Dressage Champs."

"We're not good enough for that," Lizzie said.

"Spud is good enough," Jane said. "And if you keep on improving the way you have done so far, you'll be good enough too. You should go in for the Junior Mount and Rider competition at Riding Club too. Good practice for you."

Lizzie was silent. Sarah had been going on non-stop about Junior Mount and Rider. She was determined to win it on Melody. Several other girls from Riding Club were also going in for it, but everyone knew Melody was the best pony. And Sarah had all the right gear. Lizzie knew there were some special things you had to have for your horse, and the rider had to be immaculately dressed too, in hacking jacket, waistcoat, smart jods and ankle boots. The better quality all this equipment was, the more chance you had of winning, Sarah said. The winner of the Riding Club competition went on to represent the club at Interclub.

Mum had already taken Lizzie to the saddler's where they had bought a secondhand pair of jodhpurs and some ankle boots which were really too large. Lizzie had to wear two pairs of socks to make them fit. They also bought a brand-new shiny white helmet, which the assistant called a stack hat. While Mum was paying, Lizzie looked at some of the hacking jackets. They were astonishingly expensive. And you had to wear a velvet riding hat with them, not a white stack hat, even if it was brand-new.

"Mum and Dad can't afford to buy all the gear," she tried to explain to Jane.

Jane made a sympathetic face. "Just start going to Riding Club," she said. "Then you'll be qualified to compete anyway. We'll see what happens."

Every week there was either a training day or a competition. Lizzie did not do particularly well in any of them. Spud was not a natural jumper and would refuse anything he didn't like the look of. In novelties he was safe and accurate, but not very fast. And Lizzie was still too inexperienced to know how to ride him with complete confidence. But he did well on the dressage training day. Even though Lizzie forgot part of the test she still had the second highest score in the juniors, even higher than Sarah and Melody.

She took the dressage test results with her when she went to see Moya in hospital.

"He's got some really high marks," Moya said. "That's brilliant!" She looked thinner than ever, though her eyes were still bright and cheerful.

Lizzie was drawing a picture of Spud on Moya's cast. "Jane wants me to go in for the Junior Mount and Rider competition," she said. "Do you think I should?"

"It's up to you," Moya said, with a strange look on her face, as if she was trying not to say something. And then she said it in a rush: "Lizzie, Spud's never won anything. I would just love it if he won a blue ribbon. It would mean so much to me." Then she added, "But I don't want you to do anything you don't feel ready for."

Mum usually came to Riding Club to watch, and sometimes Dad came too.

"Is Lizzie going in for Junior Mount and Rider?" Mrs Chapman asked Mum one Sunday, when both she and Dad were there.

"I'm not sure we can get all the gear," Mum said. "She may have to miss out this year."

"What a shame," Mrs Chapman said. "Sarah would love to lend Lizzie some things, but of course the rules say you aren't allowed to ride with borrowed equipment."

Dad's face darkened.

"That's rather a mean rule," he said later. "Why shouldn't Lizzie have a shot at this Junior whatever it is if she wants to?"

Mrs Chapman always irritated Lizzie's

father into wanting to compete with her. Two days later he came home with a huge grin on his face, and a big parcel under his arm.

Lizzie was sitting at the kitchen table trying to catch up with some homework.

"I've got something for you, Lizzie," Dad crowed. He opened the parcel and drew out something made of a very funny coloured tweed. He held it up to Lizzie. It was a small hacking jacket.

Lizzie jumped up to try it on.

"And look!" Dad pulled something else out of the bag. It was a riding hat, covered in the same mustardy-green material. Lizzie stuck it on her head. It came down almost as far as her eyes.

"Where on earth did you find that?" Mum said.

"I had to go over to Salisbury to see someone and I stopped at the saddler's on the way home. Thirty dollars for both of them! What do you think?"

"It's great!" Lizzie said. "Now all I need are the things for Spud. I've got everything else. Thanks, Dad."

Mum opened her mouth to say something and then closed it again. She frowned at the hacking jacket.

"Don't you like it, Mum?" Lizzie asked.

"I do like it. It's fine. It's just – I've never seen a green one before. Most of the girls wear grey or navy, don't they?"

"I don't care what colour it is," Lizzie said. "Just as long as I've got it. Now I can take Spud in the Junior Mount and Rider."

By the time Lizzie rode down to the Club on the morning of the competition she was too exhausted to feel excited. She had spent the day before washing Spud and cleaning her tack until everything shone. Moya, home from hospital but still on crutches, had dug out some of the other things she needed, like a lanyard and a Spanish martingale. Lizzie had got up at five o'clock in the morning to plait Spud's mane. Jane had shown her how to plait, but she had never done it on her own before. She had no idea it would take so long. When Mum came out at seven to tell her breakfast was ready, only half Spud's mane was done and Lizzie was nearly in tears.

Mum had helped finish off the plaits, but she had never plaited a mane before either, and the plaits weren't anything like as neat and straight as they should have been.

But we look smarter than we've ever looked before, Lizzie thought, trying to cheer herself up. Spud's been doing the practice tests really well. And it's not as if I'm really expecting to get anywhere.

Spud stepped out eagerly, his ears forward. It was a beautiful spring day and as always when she was riding Lizzie began to feel light-hearted.

But when they arrived at the Club grounds her spirits fell. The other riders and horses were almost unrecognizable. The riders all looked so smart and the horses gleamed. Their manes were in tiny neat plaits, not like Spud's big wobbly lumps. And some of them had been clipped to a smooth sheen. Next to them, despite all her washing and grooming, Spud looked really scruffy in his shaggy winter coat.

By the gate to the Club there was a space for horse trailers. Melody was tied up alongside a brand-new trailer.

Sarah was taking off the pony's travelling boots. Melody looked shining and spotless, and everything Sarah wore was brand-new.

"Is that your trailer?" Lizzie asked.

"Yes, we got it last week. If I'm going to go to shows Mum said we needed one."

"Wow," Lizzie said.

"Mum didn't want me to ride down today in case Melody got dirty," Sarah added.

"Melody looks wonderful!" Lizzie said. "However did you get her so clean?"

"Mum and I spent all day yesterday washing her," Sarah replied. "It's hard when you've got a grey." She looked up. "What on earth are you wearing?"

"It's a hacking jacket," Lizzie said, her spirits falling even further. "Dad got it for me."

"Weird colour! Like the hat too!"

"Oh well," Lizzie said, "it's not as though I've got a chance."

"No, I suppose not," Sarah agreed.

Mrs Chapman came bustling over. "Better get on, Sarah, they're about to start. Oh, you've got your boots muddy. Here, let me clean them for you. Now stand on this towel, not on the grass." She fussed over Sarah and then caught sight of Lizzie. "Hello dear, your pony looks nice. You must let me help you plait next time. I think I've got the hang of it now. How clever of your mother to make a hat to match the jacket. I've never seen one like that before."

Lizzie rode to join the line of horses, her face on fire. She thought of all the work she had put into getting ready. She could see everyone else looked much smarter than she and Spud did. She must look really stupid next to them all.

Oh why had she decided to go in for the competition? Spud was a marvellous horse. She didn't need to wear the right clothes to make him any better. She wished she was at home, riding him in the paddock, not at this horrible competition.

After the judges had inspected each horse and rider, the competitors had to do a test which involved both trotting and cantering over poles. Lizzie had practised it several times with Jane.

"It's not easy for Spud," Jane had said. "The test is more for ponies and his canter stride is too long for the poles. You'll have to hold him in and make him canter really slowly, otherwise he'll hit the poles and lose marks."

Lizzie was last to ride. Most of the ponies had done the test well. It would be hard to choose between them. She knew she had no hope of winning, but she wanted Spud to go well. She so much wanted people to notice him and realize how special he was. As she was warming up she caught sight of Dad who had just arrived with Moya. She wondered if she would ever win a ribbon for Moya.

She rode into the arena and bowed to the

judge. Then she began the trot circles. She thought Spud was moving well and she began to relax. But when she had to canter, disaster struck. Spud did a clumsy transition and threw her forward and her hat fell right over her eyes.

She was supposed to canter him over the poles and she couldn't see where they were! She put one hand up to push the hat back and Spud speeded up a bit. The hat fell forward again. Spud looked at the poles and decided they were jumps. He jumped nimbly over each one.

By this time he was moving quite fast and Lizzie still couldn't see. The turn came up much faster than she expected and neither she nor Spud were ready for it. Spud made a neat leap sideways and they found themselves outside the competition area.

The judge's bell rang. It meant elimination.

Lizzie was sure everyone was laughing. She thought she heard someone say, "That horse is far too big for that little girl." And then Mrs Chapman said loudly, "Poor Lizzie. She's only just started having lessons, you know. I think it was a bit too soon for her to try competing."

Lizzie rode quietly over to the hitching rail and slid down from Spud's back. She took off his bridle and put on his halter. Then she started undoing the plaits. Mum came over and stood next to her. They both undid plaits for a few moments without saying anything.

"That was bad luck," Mum said. "Are you OK?"

Lizzie sniffed. "I let him down. I should have ridden him better."

"You rode really well," Mum said. "And when he came in I heard one of the girls' fathers say, "Now that's a nice looking horse!"

"Just a hopeless rider," Lizzie groaned.

"There'll be lots of other competitions," Mum said. "This was your first one, after all. And you've only just started riding. You can't expect to win."

"I didn't expect to win," Lizzie said fiercely. "I knew I wouldn't. I haven't got any of the right gear. Not like Sarah."

"I don't know much about horses," Mum said quietly, "but I'd have thought having the right gear was the least important part."

Lizzie knew her mother was right, but even though she didn't want to win, she did want everyone to see how special Spud was.

Moya limped over, followed attentively by Dad.

"I didn't know you could ride like that," Dad said.

"I was eliminated!" Lizzie exclaimed.

"Yes, but you looked really good up till that point," Dad replied. "And you stayed on, which was more than I would have done."

"You did look nice," Moya said. "And Spud looks beautiful. I was really proud of both of you."

But I didn't win you a ribbon, Lizzie thought. And I don't suppose I ever will.

Presentation time came. Nine riders had competed and the list was read from the bottom up. Of course, Lizzie's name wasn't mentioned as she had been eliminated. Finally it was the last two. Sarah's name still hadn't been read out. Lizzie looked across at Sarah and her mother. Their faces were tense with anxiety. It means so much to them to win, she realized. But did they want people to see Melody as a special little horse, or did they just want to win?

Second place went to a girl called Emma. She laughed ruefully as she went to collect her ribbon. Then Sarah rode up, a wide smile transforming her face, to receive her sash and a trophy. Lizzie ran over to congratulate her.

"That was such bad luck for you," Sarah said. "Poor old Spud!"

"Well, it's not as if he's Lizzie's own pony," Mrs Chapman said, meaning to cheer her up but doing quite the opposite. "It's lovely for you to have something to ride, dear, but he is a bit big for you, isn't he?"

He's not too big for me! And he's not poor old Spud, Lizzie thought angrily. So what if Spud wasn't really hers. She and Spud and Moya were all part of a team. But how was she ever going to show people how special Spud was?

Chapter eight

"Never mind!" Jane said later. "There's still the Dressage Champs."

"I'm not sure I want to go to any more competitions," Lizzie said. "I haven't got any of the right clothes, and I just make a fool of myself."

"Everyone makes a fool of themselves sooner or later where horses are concerned," Jane laughed. "Did I ever tell you how I fell off Charlie at the water jump? In front of hundreds of people. I was in the lead too!

"Spud's so good," she went on. "It's a waste

not to be competing him. It was such a stroke of luck to get him. Most people would give an arm and a leg for a horse like Spud. And you're a natural dressage rider."

Hearing this cheered Lizzie up, but she couldn't help feeling Jane was exaggerating.

However, Jane made her send in the entry form, and offered to take Spud in her trailer.

When the programme arrived Lizzie looked at it in awe. There was Spud's name, Pure Chance, and there was her name, Elizabeth Bain. She showed the programme to Mum who was similarly impressed. Later that day they drove into the city and went to see Moya in her little flat.

Moya stared at Pure Chance's name. "It's wonderful," she said. "It's like a dream come true."

She picked up her crutches and hobbled over to the bureau. From one of its drawers she took out a small package wrapped in tissue paper.

"Here, Lizzie," she said, "I bought these years ago when I still thought I might compete on Spud one day. I want you to have them and wear them at the Champs."

Inside were a pale grey tie and a pair of fawn leather riding gloves. Lizzie pulled the gloves on. They fitted her perfectly.

"The only trouble is, they don't really go with the green jacket Dad got me," Lizzie said reluctantly to Mum in the car.

"I know," Mum said, "that's why we're going home this way. We'll stop in at the saddler's and see if we can get you a velvet hat that fits you properly and maybe even a hacking jacket to go with the tie!"

"Mum!" Lizzie exclaimed, thrilled. "Can we afford it?"

"An extraordinary thing happened," Mum

replied. "Mrs Chapman asked me to do a portrait of Melody. I think I might have a whole new career doing pictures of horses."

The next horse in Arena D, the Young Rider Preliminary, is Pure Chance, ridden by Elizabeth Bain.

Lizzie's heart skipped a beat when she heard her name echoing over the showground from the loudspeakers. And Spud's name too. Pure Chance. It sounded so grand.

What a good name it is for him, Lizzie thought, it was pure chance that I got him, pure chance that we're here today.

Spud looked beautiful. Lizzie had brushed him for an hour every day for the last few weeks, until his winter coat had all come out. His summer coat was bright and smooth and his white socks gleamed. Jane had shown her how to pull his mane, and his plaits looked small and neat, showing off the lovely curve of his neck. He felt good too, very light and responsive. His neck arched as he carried himself, and she could feel the movement and the swing coming from behind.

"I'm going to do my best for you," she promised him. "I won't let you down this time."

She patted the pocket of her new hacking jacket where she was carrying her lucky hoof pick.

When the girl in front of her had left the arena, Lizzie rode Spud up to where the judges sat in their cars. One judge was a man, the other a woman. They both gave Lizzie really warm smiles and told her to have a nice ride. She went to the end of the arena and began to trot Spud in circles, waiting to hear the bell.

It seemed to take ages before it rang. She

was just wondering if it had already rung and she hadn't heard it, when it did ring. She completed the circle and entered the arena. Spud moved beneath her with his big, flowing gait.

"Think *Halt*," Lizzie told herself, and Spud came to a perfect square halt at exactly the right spot. She bowed her head to each of the judges and then trotted on.

The test took about six minutes to ride. It was a very simple one, with straightforward movements, trot circles followed by canter circles, crossing the diagonal at a free rein walk and at sit trot, with another final halt at X. Lizzie could feel Spud was going well. He was relaxed and calm, yet his steps were energetic and always forward. The circles seemed to be a good shape and whenever they had to do the movement on a marker, they always hit the spot perfectly.

When Spud came to another square halt

and Lizzie saluted the judges again, she felt like throwing her arms round his neck. She had to content herself with giving him a big pat as they left the arena, Spud walking out with long relaxed steps.

There was a little flutter of applause and Lizzie saw Mum and Dad, Jane and Moya. Even Neil and Scott had come to watch. She grinned at them. They surrounded her as she walked Spud back to the trailer.

"Very nice," Jane said. "I've never seen him go so well."

"He was marvellous," Moya said.

"That was cool!" Scott praised her.

"It was fantastic," Neil added. "Not that I know the first thing about it!"

Mum helped Lizzie take off Spud's saddle and bridle. Lizzie gave him a carrot. Then she did put her arms round his neck and hugged him. Spud nuzzled her.

"Let's go and look at the scores," Jane said.

"I'll stay here with Spud for a bit." Lizzie couldn't bear the idea of having to look at the scoreboard. She had been on almost last in her class. There were twenty other riders. Sarah and Melody, looking perfectly turned out as usual, had done a good test and were lying second at the moment, behind a very young looking girl whose mother was a champion rider. Lizzie knew Spud had done a nice test. Was it nice enough for a place, though?

Everyone else went to look at the scores. Only Moya stayed with Lizzie. They got a cold drink out of the ice box and sat down. Spud was munching on the lucerne in his hay net. Neither of them could stop staring at him.

"Thank you, Lizzie," Moya said quietly. "I'm so happy to see Spud happy."

"Thank you for lending him to me," Lizzie said. She wanted to tell Moya how grateful she was, but she found it hard to put into words.

Then Jane came running up, her face red with excitement, her blue eyes blazing.

"You'd better get Spud ready again, kiddo," she panted.

"Why?" Lizzie said.

"You've got to get ready for the presentation. You've got the highest score on the board. You've won!"

As Lizzie rode towards the presentation area she saw Sarah just ahead of her. She made Spud trot so they could catch up.

"Well done!" Sarah said. "That was pretty amazing!"

Lizzie took the hoof pick out of her pocket. "Do you remember when we found this in the shed? Neither of us had a pony then – and now we both do. Even though Spud isn't really mine," she added quickly.

The presentation went by in a dream. Luckily Dad took dozens of photos from every angle, otherwise Lizzie would never have believed it had really happened. She rode Spud back to the float, the blue sash round his neck. Sarah and Melody followed with their white sash for third place. Jane brought them the test papers to read.

Everyone crowded round to look at them. Lizzie's marks were all sevens and eights. *Lovely paces* was one comment, *Very nicely ridden* another.

"David Reid said he had lovely paces," Jane said. "See, I always told you he was special."

"Who's David Reid?" Lizzie asked.

"He was one of your judges. He's a top dressage instructor."

"Spud," Dad said, "I'm sorry I ever doubted you. I'm proud of you, my boy."

"What about Lizzie?" Mum said. "Aren't you proud of her too?"

"She just sits there," Dad replied, with a twinkle in his eye. "Spud does all the work!"

"Don't you believe it," Jane said. "Lizzie's a very good rider and she's worked very hard."

"I know!" Dad gave Lizzie a big hug. "Well done," he said. "Looks like you finally found your thing!"

"Congratulations, Jane," a voice spoke behind them. "Your students did well."

Lizzie recognized the judge, David Reid.

"That's a very nice horse," he went on, patting Spud on the neck. "He wouldn't be for sale would he? I'm looking for something for one of my students."

"You'd have to ask Moya," Jane said. "She's his owner."

The Bains all turned to look at Moya. Even Dad looked horrified at the thought of Spud being sold. Lizzie went cold.

Moya said, "He's not for sale. Actually he's not really mine any more. You see, I'd just decided to give him to Lizzie."

"Well, they make a good combination," David Reid said smiling. "He's certainly a very special horse. How did you come to find him, Lizzie?"

Lizzie looked at Spud, his blue sash bright against his bay coat. For a moment she was speechless. Everyone had seen how special Spud was. And this beautiful little horse was going to be hers. She couldn't stop grinning.

"It was pure chance," she said.

She undid the blue sash and gave it to Moya. "Pure chance."